W9-DGH-814

DEC 2 2 2012

The DINOSAUR Files
PLANT-EATERS

text *by* Olivia Brookes

WINDMILL
BOOKS ™

New York

Published in 2012 by Windmill Books, an imprint of Rosen Publishing
29 East 21st Street, New York, NY 10010

Illustrated by Julius T. Csotonyi, Steve Kirk, Simon Mendez,
Eric Robson, Peter Scott, John Sibbick, Studio Inklink, and David Wright
Illustration copyright © Julius T. Csotonyi 8TR
Illustration copyright © John Sibbick 6B, 13TL

Library of Congress Cataloging-in-Publication Data

Brookes, Olivia.
Plant-eaters / by Olivia Brookes.
p. cm. — (The dinosaur files)
Includes index.
ISBN 978-1-61533-517-6 (library binding) — ISBN 978-1-61533-522-0 (pbk.)
— ISBN 978-1-61533-523-7 (6-pack)
1. Dinosaurs—Juvenile literature. 2. Herbivores—Juvenile literature. I. Title.
QE861.5.B7566 2012
567.9-dc23
2011022837

Printed and bound in Malaysia

Websites
For Web resources related to the subject of this book,
go to: www.windmillbooks.com/weblinks
and select this book's title.

CPSIA Compliance Information: Batch #OW2102WM: For further information contact Windmill Books, New York, New York at
1-866-478-0556.

Contents

THE FIRST DINOSAURS were meat-eaters. But other kinds soon evolved to take advantage of the plentiful vegetation. The first plant-eaters were the prosauropods. Like the meat-eaters, they also walked on two legs. But, as time went on, they became longer and bulkier, so they walked on all fours. The sauropods, which evolved in the Jurassic, included giants such as Diplodocus, Apatosaurus, and Brachiosaurus. They were the largest animals ever to walk on land.

The sauropods were joined by other kinds of plant-eaters, including the stegosaurs, dinosaurs with plates and spines on their backs, and ankylosaurs, dinosaurs with bony armor that covered their bodies.

With no ability to chew their food, sauropods relied on pebbles that they had swallowed to grind up the vegetation in their stomachs to help with digestion. Still other kinds of plant-eaters, the ornithopods, had jaws that could grind up food in their mouths. The ornithopods became the dominant plant-eaters of the Cretaceous. The sauropods, meanwhile, died out everywhere except in South America.

Plateosaurus

PLATEOSAURUS walked sometimes on on its hind legs, other times on all fours. It had short arms, but its long neck made it easy to reach leaves on high branches. Its strong jaws were full of small, sharp, leaf-shaped teeth.

With eyes on both sides of its small head, it could see all around when looking for food or watching for enemies.

If attacked, Plateosaurus rose up on its back legs. It could fight back using the sharp claws on its thumbs and toes. Its heavy tail was a useful weapon, too.

Plateosaurus was 30 ft (9 m) long and 8 ft (2.4 m) tall.

BURIED DEEP BELOW

Plateosaurus means "flat-lizard." It gets its name from the flat shape of the first Plateosaurus fossils found in 1834. Scientists think that Plateosauruses were very common dinosaurs because so many of their fossils have been found in the dry regions of Europe where they lived.

In 1997, Plateosaurus fossil bones were found in rocks more than a mile below the surface of the North Sea. This is the deepest place dinosaur fossils have ever been discovered.

Massospondylus (above) was too heavy to walk upright. It had a long neck so it could still reach leaves on trees. Mussaurus (below) means "mouse lizard" because the first tiny fossils found were only hatchlings.

Riojasaurus (right) lived in the deserts of South America. Like its cousin Plateosaurus, it had clawed toes.

Riojasaurus

Mussaurus

D IPLODOCUS had a large, stocky body with pillar-like legs and spikes that ran down its back. Its front legs were shorter than its back legs. Using its long neck, it could easily reach its favorite foods: leaves, ferns, and water plants. It had a long, whip-like tail, good for defense against predators.

Diplodocus had peg-shaped teeth at the front of its mouth. These were perfect for stripping leaves off branches.

Diplodocuses were fully grown at just 10 years old.

Diplodocus was 90 ft (27 m) long

Diplodocus's long neck was useful for scaring enemies or showing off to females.

LIGHT, LONG, AND LOUD

Diplodocus's name means "double beam" because of the shape of the bones inside its tail. It is the longest dinosaur known to scientists for which a complete skeleton has been found. Diplodocus might have used its long tail for protection. It could swing it at attackers or crack it like a whip to scare them. Even though it was very long and large, Diplodocus weighed only as much as three elephants.

Shunosaurus had a spiny club at the end of its tail.

Both Diplodocus and its relative Barosaurus (below) had necks more than 20 ft (6 m) long. They may have had not one but eight hearts linked together. Each helped to pump blood all the way up to the head.

TWINKLE TOES

Believe it or not, Diplodocus walked around on tiptoe! It had wide feet with a round heel bone padded by a ball of flesh the size of a basketball. One of its toes had a large claw.

Amargasaurus (above) one of Diplodocus's relatives, had long spines on its neck.

Stegosaurus

STEGOSAURUS had a bulky body with a high, arched back and stocky limbs. It walked with its small head low to the ground and its spiked tail held high. It is probably best known for the double row of broad plates on its back. Stegosaurus used its great sense of smell to find its favorite foods: mosses, ferns, and low-growing conifers.

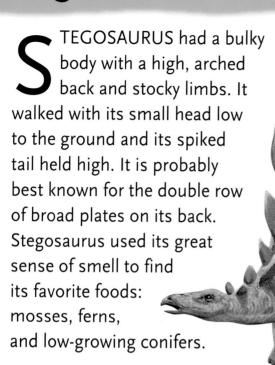

Stegosaurus's plates were good for regulating its body temperature, attracting a mate, and scaring enemies.

Though it was a gentle plant-eater, Stegosaurus could put up a fight when danger appeared. Turning its back on the enemy, it would swing its spiked tail into its head.

Stegosaurus was 30 ft (9 m) long and 13 ft (4 m) tall.

ROOF LIZARD

The name Stegosaurus means "roof lizard." This is because scientists once wrongly thought that its plates laid flat along its back, overlapping like roof tiles, instead of standing up. The plates probably helped control Stegosaurus's body temperature. The blood vessels inside each plate would take in heat when the dinosaur needed to warm up, or give off heat when it needed to cool off. Males might have also shown off the size or color of their plates to attract females during mating.

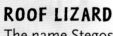

An ancestor of Stegosaurus, Scutellosaurus (above) had hundreds of bony scales all over its body. It was one of the first dinosaurs to have armor.

WALNUT BRAIN

Stegosaurus's brain was only the size of a walnut. It had tiny teeth and could not chew its food. Instead, it had to swallow stones that would grind up food inside its stomach.

Brachiosaurus

BRACHIOSAURUS was a huge, four-legged sauropod with a thick, fairly short tail. Like a giraffe today, it had a very long neck and its front legs were longer than its back legs. There was a high crest on its head, large nostrils above its eyes, and many chisel-like teeth in its mouth. Brachiosaurus roamed the forests of North America, eating cycad or ginkgo leaves and pine needles.

Brachiosaurus was 82 ft (25 m) long and 43 ft (13 m) tall.

A fully-grown Brachiosaurus was so big that it was safe from even the largest predators, such as Allosaurus. The little ones still had to watch out, though!

Brachiosaurus could probably stand up on its hind legs to reach the very tops of trees while eating. The bones in its long neck were hollow and not heavy to lift.

ARM LIZARD

Brachiosaurus means "arm lizard" because its front limbs were longer than its back limbs. This was unusual for a dinosaur. Because of the way it stood, Brachiosaurus could have looked through the fourth-floor window of a building. The skeleton of a close relative, Giraffatitan, in the Humboldt Museum of Berlin, Germany, is the largest mounted skeleton in the world. Brachiosaurus would have weighed between 30 and 50 tons.

A Brachiosaurus and a Ceratosaurus confront one another.

Argentinosaurus

Diplodocus

Supersaurus

Brachiosaurus

WHO WAS BIGGEST?

Brachiosaurus is the tallest and heaviest dinosaur known from a complete skeleton. But scientists have found enough bones from Argentinosaurus, a large dinosaur that lived in mid-Cretaceous Argentina, to guess that this dinosaur was most likely heavier. It probably weighed about 73 tons.

Iguanodon

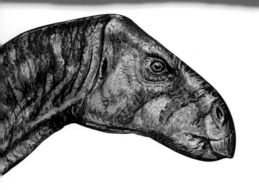

GUANODON was a large ornithopod. It had flexible arms, powerful hind legs, and a strong, flat tail. It could run very fast on two legs to escape from predators. To help it walk or run through squishy, wet swamplands its toes could be splayed wide. Iguanodon used its sharp beak and teeth to tear ferns and cycads. Its thumbs, shaped like spikes, made great defensive weapons.

Fossil tracks reveal that while Iguanodon sometimes walked on all fours, it usually walked on two feet. As it walked, it leaned forward, using its flat, stiff tail to help it balance.

Iguanodon's thumb spike was as much as 6 in (15 cm) long. It could be also used to rip open tough fruit or to tear down leaves.

Iguanodon was 30 ft (9 m) long and 10 ft (3 m) tall.

Iguanodon ate by holding leaves or twigs in its sharp beak, pulling them apart using its little finger (below). Then it ground them up with its cheek teeth. When these teeth wore out, new ones would grow in.

EARLY DISCOVERY

Iguanodon was the second dinosaur ever to be discovered, after Megalosaurus. Its fossils were first found in 1822. Its name means "iguana tooth" because its teeth are shaped like an iguana's today. Other Iguanodon fossils have given strong clues that they lived in herds.

When Iguanodon's bones were first pieced together in the 19th century, scientists thought it was a sturdy, four-legged, bear-like animal with a spike on its nose. Later, it was thought the bones should be arranged to make it stand up like a kangaroo. Nowadays, scientists agree that Iguanodon stood with its backbone horizontal.

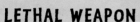

LETHAL WEAPON

If a large, hungry theropod attacked, and there was nowhere to run, Iguanodon could use its long thumb spike to defend itself by stabbing its enemy's body. The spike was strong enough to pierce even the toughest skin.

Hypsilophodon

Hypsilophodon sheared off leaves or plants with its beak and stuffed them into its cheek pouches. When old teeth wore out, new ones grew in.

HYPSILOPHODON was like a modern mammal: a gazelle. It could run very fast on its two long, slender legs. It had very large eyes, good for keeping a lookout for predators. Its two short arms each had five clawed fingers. It also had a long, stiff tail that probably helped it balance as it sprinted away from trouble at high speed.

KEEPING WATCH
Hypsilophodon gathered in herds and spent their days nibbling low-growing plants on open plains. While most ate, some kept watch for danger.

Under threat from its enemies, Hypsilophodon's only choice was to run, and run fast.

"LITTLE LIZARD"
Xiaosaurus (left) lived in China during the mid-Jurassic period. It was just 5 ft (1.5 m) long but had similar features to Hypsilophodon: large eyes, a long, stiff tail, and it and ran on two long, slim legs.

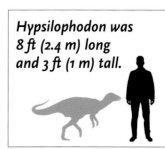

Hypsilophodon was 8 ft (2.4 m) long and 3 ft (1 m) tall.

LIVED AND DIED TOGETHER

Hypsilophodon means "high ridge tooth." It is named for its high-crowned, grooved cheek teeth.

The remains of 24 Hypsilophodon were once found in the same place. This probably means that an entire herd died together after becoming stuck in quicksand.

Camptosaurus (above) was a 20-ft (6 m) long ornithopod. It was an ancestor of the Hypsilophodon family.

AMBUSH VICTIM

Tenontosaurus (above) was once believed to be a very large member of the Hypsilophodon family. Now scientists think it is a more distant relative. Its fossil remains were discovered along with fossils of several Deinonychus, which are known to have hunted in packs. Poor Tenontosaurus was most likely the victim of an ambush by these fierce pack-hunters.

Euoplocephalus

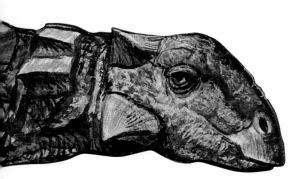

EUOPLOCEPHALUS was an armored dinosaur. It had a stocky, low-slung body, stout legs, and clawed feet. Plates of spiked, bony armor were found in the skin on its neck, back, tail, and even in its eyelids! It had large spines on its shoulders and a heavy club at the end of its tail.

Ankylosaurus (left) was an armored dinosaur known for its clubbed tail and the smooth, rounded knobs of bone covering its back.

Unlike Ankylosaurus, Euoplocephalus (left) had sharp spikes around its head and shoulders. Both had clubbed tails.

Euoplocephalus was 20 ft (6 m) long and 7 ft (2m) tall.

CLUBS AND ARMOR

Euopleocephalus means "well-armored head." It got this name because of the bony spikes on its head. Even though it was nearly fully armored, it was still vulnerable to attack from predators. So it most likely roamed in herds for safety in numbers.

BIG TAIL, BIG NOSE

The name Talarurus means "basket tail," so named for the shape of its tail club. Talarurus had large nostrils that met at the front of its face to form one large opening. This probably helped it keep cool in the deserts where it lived.

Ankylosaurs like Euoplocephalus, Ankylosaurus, Saichania (above), and Talarurus (below right) all had a defensive weapon: a large ball of bone at the ends of their tails. They used it to swing at their enemies, such as Tarbosaurus (below left).

Styracosaurus

STYRACOSAURUS had a long nose horn on its toothless beak and small horns on each cheek. Its stocky body was like a rhinoceros's. Six long spikes and some smaller knobs of bone stuck out from the edge of its neck frill. This frill helped keep the dinosaur's body temperature low. It probably also looked quite scary to its enemies. The colors on the frill's skin may have helped attract a mate.

Styracosaurus's frill was not solid bone but had wide openings covered in skin.

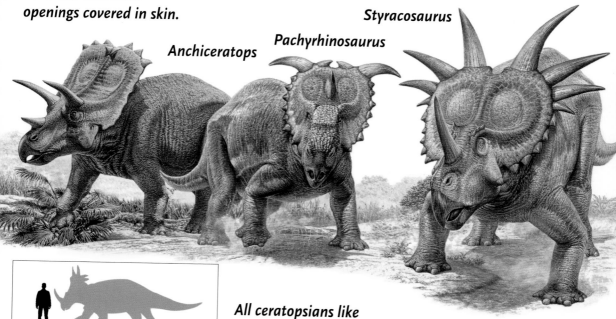

Anchiceratops

Pachyrhinosaurus

Styracosaurus

Styracosaurus was 18 ft (5 m) long and 6 ft (1.8 m) tall.

All ceratopsians like Styracosaurus had a similar body shape: massive head with horn or horns, toothless beaks, neck frills and sturdy, pillar-like legs.

CALL ME "SPIKE"

The name Styracosaurus means "spiked lizard." It was named for the spikes on its frill. The longest was 20 inches (51 cm) long, about the length of an adult human's arm. The frill may have changed color during courtship.

THE LAST DINOSAURS

Ceratopsians were one of the last groups of dinosaurs to evolve before all dinosaurs became extinct at the end of the Cretaceous period. They had chopping teeth, good for chewing the toughest plants. Like elephants and rhinos today, they may have been able to gallop away from danger. Scientists think they also lived together in herds for safety.

Psittacosaurus, or "parrot dinosaur," was an early Asian ceratopsian. It was named for its bony, toothless beak.

ON GUARD

Protoceratops was a 7 ft- (2 m) long ceratopsian from Mongolia. Its teeth were perfect for slicing up semi-desert plants. It laid its sausage-shaped eggs in a nest, up to 18 at a time. The eggs were about 8 inches (20 cm) long. Protoceratops was very protective of its eggs.

Centrosaurus's skeleton shows typical ceratopsian features: a gapped frill, a stocky body, and hoofed feet.

PARASAUROLOPHUS was a duck-billed dinosaur (hadrosaur). It had a long face, a flat snout, and a toothless beak. It walked on its two strong hind legs. Parasaurolophus's most distinctive feature was its long, bony, hollow crest. Its skull alone was 6 ft (1.8 m) long, the height of an adult human!

Parasaurolophus fed on conifer needles and magnolia leaves.

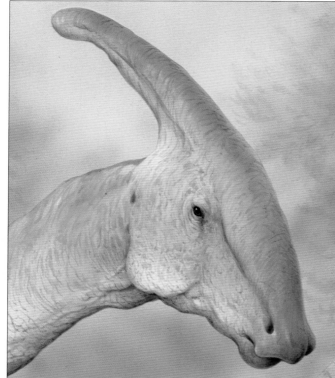

A CREST IS GOOD FOR ...

Getting attention, mainly. It had hollow tubes inside linked to the nose and could make deep bellowing sounds. These were good for impressing mates, warning off rivals, or sounding an alarm when danger appeared. The crest may also have helped the dinosaur keep a cool head by letting off heat from the brain.

Parasaurolophus was 30 ft (9 m) long and 10 ft (3 m) tall.

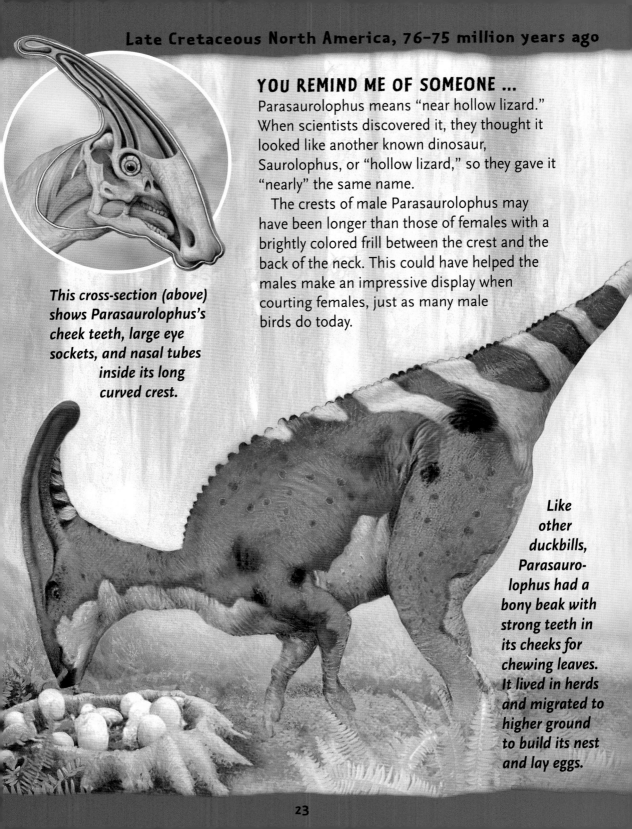

YOU REMIND ME OF SOMEONE ...

Parasaurolophus means "near hollow lizard." When scientists discovered it, they thought it looked like another known dinosaur, Saurolophus, or "hollow lizard," so they gave it "nearly" the same name.

The crests of male Parasaurolophus may have been longer than those of females with a brightly colored frill between the crest and the back of the neck. This could have helped the males make an impressive display when courting females, just as many male birds do today.

This cross-section (above) shows Parasaurolophus's cheek teeth, large eye sockets, and nasal tubes inside its long curved crest.

Like other duckbills, Parasaurolophus had a bony beak with strong teeth in its cheeks for chewing leaves. It lived in herds and migrated to higher ground to build its nest and lay eggs.

Lambeosaurus

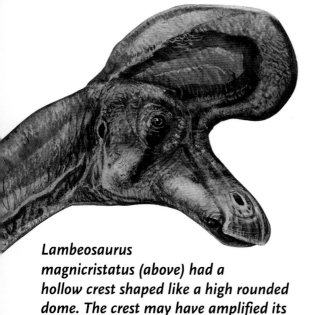

Lambeosaurus magnicristatus (above) had a hollow crest shaped like a high rounded dome. The crest may have amplified its bellowing warning calls.

LAMBEOSAURUS was a type of duck-billed dinosaur (hadrosaur). It had a flat, tootless beak and a U-shaped neck. It walked through swampy woodlands on its long hind legs, feeding on leaves. Its short front legs had fleshy padded hooves. Its tail was wide and stiff. Different species of Lambeosaurus had different crest shapes: some were hatchet-shaped, while others were high and round.

Lambeosaurus lambei's crest was hatchet-shaped. Corythosaurus's was curved.

Lambeosaurus lambei

Lambeosaurus was 30 ft (9m) long and 10 ft (3 m) tall.

SNORKELS ...

Lambeosaurus was named for the Canadian geologist, Lawrence Lamb, who was the first person to study it. It was once thought that crested hadrosaurs like Lambeosaurus were aquatic animals that used their crests like snorkels or oxygen tanks to breathe underwater.

... AND HELMETS

The name Corythosaurus means "helmet lizard," so named for the shape of its crest. Like Lambeosaurus, its crest contained nasal tubes that may have allowed it to make loud, deep warning or mating calls.

Hadrosaurs had hundreds of teeth. When old, worn teeth fell out, new ones grew in. Hadrosaurs could chew up tough plants very well and had long twisted intestines (above), which helped digestion.

Baby hadrosaurs hatch out of their eggs. They are like miniature adults, able to walk immediately.

Maiasaura was a duck-billed dinosaur (hadrosaur). It had a long snout, a toothless beak, and crests above its eyes. Inside its cheeks were many self-sharpening teeth, perfect for grinding up plants, berries, leaves, and seeds. Its scaly skin was covered with warts. Like other hadrosaurs, it walked sometimes on two legs, other times on all fours. Its back legs were longer and stronger than the front ones. Its toes had fleshy pads on their undersides.

Maiasaura feeds her babies.

Fossil remains of Maiasaura were discovered along with those of nests, eggshells, and hatchlings. The hatchlings' cute appearance (large head and eyes) made the mother Maiasaura feel maternal towards her brood!

Maiasaura was 30 ft (9 m) long and 10 ft (3 m) tall.

DINOSAUR ASTRONAUT

Maiasaura means "good mother lizard." It was so named because of the evidence that it reared its hatchlings.

Maiasaura was the first dinosaur in space! A fragment of bone and a piece of eggshell flew with American astronaut Loren Acton on an eight-day shuttle mission in 1985.

LAST MEAL

Edmontosaurus (left) was a close relative of Maiasaura. Scientists have discovered how this hadrosaur lived by studying its fossilized skin and the food inside its stomach when it died.

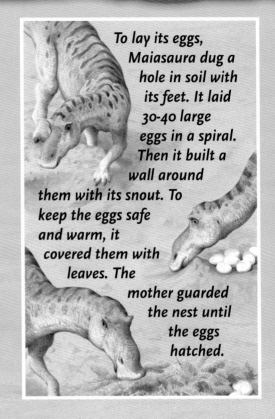

To lay its eggs, Maiasaura dug a hole in soil with its feet. It laid 30-40 large eggs in a spiral. Then it built a wall around them with its snout. To keep the eggs safe and warm, it covered them with leaves. The mother guarded the nest until the eggs hatched.

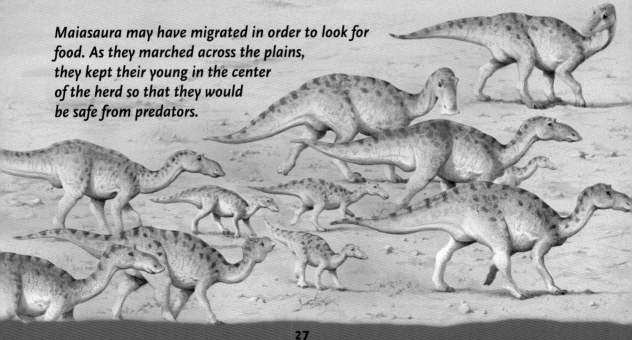

Maiasaura may have migrated in order to look for food. As they marched across the plains, they kept their young in the center of the herd so that they would be safe from predators.

Pachycephalosaurus

pak-ee-sef-uh-luh-SAWR-us

PACHYCEPHALO-SAURUS walked on its hind legs. Its thick, stiff tail helped its balance. It had short, stubby arms with clawed fingers. Its smooth, domed skull had bony knobs just above its stocky neck. There were also short, bony spikes on its snout. It chewed leaves and fruit with its tiny cheek teeth.

Just as rams and billy goats use their horns for fighting today, the thick, domed skulls of Pachycephalosaurus and its relatives may have been used for contests between rival males during the breeding season.

Pachycephalosaurus was 15 ft (5 m) long and 7 ft (2 m) tall.

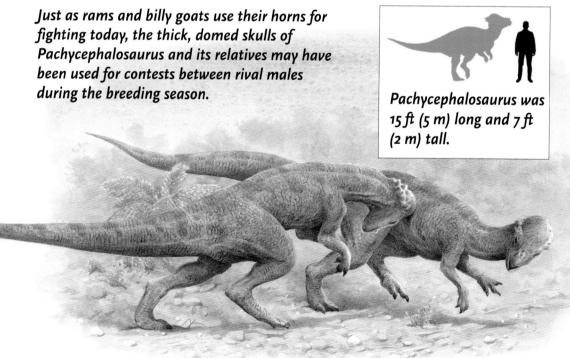

THICK BUT SENSITIVE

Pachycephalosaurus means "thick-headed lizard." It was named for its domed skull. Scientists think it probably had a very good sense of sight and smell. These helped it spot predators in time to make its escape. It ran on two legs, leaning forward with its head and heavy tail held level.

YOUR NAME IS — WHAT?!

Fossil remains of Stygimoloch (below) were first found among the Hell Creek rock formations in Montana. Its name means "horned devil from the river of death." It was named for where it was found, and for the scary 6-inch (15 cm) spikes on its head.

Stegoceras—no, not Stegosaurus—was a close relative of Pachycephalosaurus, only it was about half the size of its cousin. As Stegoceras (above) grew older, the dome on its head grew over the bony rim around the sides and back of its head, just like a top hat.

Triceratops

TRICERATOPS had a massive head with a long snout. Its neck frill was made of solid bone. It had two long horns over its eyes and one shorter one just behind its parrot-like beak. Inside its mouth were hundreds of sharp teeth used for grinding down tough plants and leaves. The skin covering its huge body was tough. Triceratops was so big that most predators would have shied away from attacking it.

Triceratops was 30 ft (9 m) long and 8 ft (2.4 m) tall.

Threatened by attack from a Tyrannosaurus, Triceratops stood its ground and tried to look as mean and fierce possible. It lowered its head to show off its neck frill and horns.

PIECE BY PIECE

The name Triceratops means "three-horned face." What we know about Triceratops has been pieced together from hundreds of fossil pieces. A complete skeleton has never been found.

HEAVY FRILL

Only Triceratops had a frill that was made of solid bone. Its relatives had gaps in their frills covered with skin, which made them lighter. Triceratops's neck frill was over 6 feet (1.8 m) long. Together with its snout, its colossal head was more than one-third the length of its whole body.

Two Triceratops take a drink.

Glossary and Index

ankylosaurs (ANG-kuh-loh-sawrz) Dinosaurs fully covered in armored plates, studs, and spikes. Some had tail clubs.

ceratopsians (ser-uh-TOP-see-unz) Horned dinosaurs. Some, like Triceratops, had huge neck frills and narrow beaks.

dinosaurs (DY-nuh-sawrz) Reptiles that lived on land 230-65 million years ago and walked upright on legs held beneath their bodies.

evolution (eh-vuh-LOO-shun) The process by which forms of life gradually change over millions of years.

fossil (FO-sul) The remains of an animal or plant preserved in rock.

hadrosaurs (HA-druh-sawrz) "Duck-billed" dinosaurs. They were plant-eaters with grinding teeth.

sauropods (SOR-uh-podz) Long-necked, four-legged, plant-eating dinosaurs.

stegosaurs (STEH-guh-sawrz) Dinosaurs that had rows of plates and spikes embedded in their backs.

theropods (THIR-uh-podz) All the meat-eating dinosaurs.